Enid Blyton's
HELLO,
MR TWIDDLE!

First published 1968
This reprint 1988

Published by Dean, an imprint of
The Hamlyn Publishing Group Limited,
Michelin House,
81 Fulham Road,
London SW3 6RB,
England

ISBN 0 603 03269 9

Printed in Great Britain
at The Bath Press, Avon

Enid Blyton's
HELLO,
MR TWIDDLE!

DEAN

CONTENTS

I

MR. TWIDDLE AND THE COW

One day Mrs. Twiddle asked Mr.
Twiddle to go and fetch her brother's
cow for her.

"Albert, my brother, is going away,"
she said, "and I told him we would look
after his cow for a day or two, Twiddle.
So you go and fetch it, and we'll keep it
in the field behind the house. It will be

7

nice to have some fresh milk for nothing."

Mr. Twiddle put down his paper and got up with a sigh. There always seemed something to do just when he was nicely settled. He brushed his hair, stuffed a clean handkerchief into his pocket, and went to the door.

"Twiddle, don't forget your hat," said Mrs. Twiddle. "I believe you'd forget to take your head with you if it wasn't so firmly fixed on."

"I don't want my hat," said Mr. Twiddle.

"You *must* take your hat!" said Mrs. Twiddle firmly. "The sun is going to be hot."

So Twiddle had to take his hat. But he felt rather obstinate that morning and he made up his mind that although he had to take his hat, he wouldn't wear it. No, he'd carry it in his hand! Aha, Mrs. Twiddle, you'd be cross if you saw that!

It was a nice hat, for it was a new one. It was brown, and had a fine brown ribbon round it, tied in a bow at the side. It fitted Mr. Twiddle perfectly. Secretly Mr. Twiddle thought he looked extremely nice in his new hat, and he quite meant to put it on if he met any one. But he didn't.

He got to the field and called the cow. The cow, a gentle creature who knew him well, came to the gate at once. Mr. Twiddle tied a rope round her neck and led her off.

He hadn't gone far before his

shoelace came undone. Mr. Twiddle looked down at it. He had his hat in one hand and the cow's rope in the other. What was he to do?

"I must just hang my hat up somewhere," said Mr. Twiddle, in a dreamy voice, for he was hot and rather sleepy. He looked for something to hang his hat up on, and saw the cow's horns, looking just like the hall-pegs at home on which he always hung his hat.

Mr. Twiddle put his hat on the horns of the surprised cow. Then he knelt down and did up his shoelace, very cleverly, with one hand.

"Ha!" he said proudly, when he had finished. "Some folks may call me a stupid man—but it isn't many who could tie a lace with one hand!"

He walked on with the cow, feeling quite pleased with himself. The cow came gently after him, wearing the brown hat, looking very comical indeed. But Mr. Twiddle had forgotten all about his hat.

It wasn't until the sun shone down really hotly on his head that he felt he needed a hat. He put his hand up to his head and found no hat there. He looked at his two hands. Now what had happened to his hat? He had certainly started out with it!

"Oh, bother, bother, bother!" said Mr. Twiddle. "I must have left it on the gate where I fetched the cow!"

So back he went, the cow still following, Mr. Twiddle's hat perched up on her horns. Soon they met Mrs. Gabble, and how she laughed to see the cow!

"Sorry I can't raise my hat to you this morning," said Mr. Twiddle politely, "but I've put it somewhere and forgotten it!"

"Ho, ho, so you have!" giggled Mrs. Gabble, and she laughed till the tears ran down her cheek.

The next person Mr. Twiddle met was Dame Shoo, and she looked quite alarmed when she saw Mr. Twiddle without a hat and the cow with one.

"Just going to look for my hat, Dame Shoo," said Mr. Twiddle politely. "You know, I've left it somewhere about, and I must find it."

"Ask the cow and maybe she'll tell you where it is," said Dame Shoo with a squeal of laughter.

Mr. Twiddle looked crossly at her. "Silly woman!" he thought. "Ask the cow indeed! As if *she* could tell me where my hat is!"

Then he met Mr. Wonks, the hot-sausage man who sold ice-creams in the summer.

"Good-day, Mr. Twiddle!" said Mr. Wonks, grinning at the cow. "Hot weather for the cow, isn't it! I see you don't want her to get a headache."

Mr. Twiddle stared at him in amazement. What *could* Mr. Wonks mean?

"You must be mad, Mr. Wonks," said Mr. Twiddle, in a high and mighty voice. "Cows don't get headaches."

"No, nor sunstroke either, by the look of things!" grinned Mr. Wonks.

Mr. Twiddle said no more. He began

to think that the sun had made every
one a little mad this morning. He got
to the field-gate, but alas! there was no
hat to be seen. Mr. Twiddle was upset.
Some one must have been along and
taken it!

"My nice new hat too!" he said

mournfully. "What, oh, what, will Mrs. Twiddle say?"

He went home so upset that he didn't notice how every one laughed at the cow with the hat on. He took the cow round to the back door, to show Mrs. Twiddle, for she was fond of the gentle creature.

As soon as Mrs. Twiddle opened the door, Mr. Twiddle began to explain about his hat.

"I'm so very sorry," he said, "but somehow or other I seem to have lost my hat. Maybe it blew away—maybe some one stole it—I don't know what happened. But, anyway, I'm very sorry, my dear, and I'll go and buy a new one this very minute. I do wish I knew what had happened to it."

"If you look behind you, you'll see that the cow had more sense than you," cried his wife. "She knew how to bring a hat home, anyhow!"

Twiddle turned and looked at the cow. He saw his hat perched on her horns.

The cow opened her mouth and spoke gently.

"Moo-oo!" she said, "moo-oo!" And she waggled her head gently, asking Mr. Twiddle to take off the hat, for it annoyed her.

"Oh, the clever creature!" cried Mr. Twiddle, in the greatest delight. "Mrs. Twiddle, do you see, she has got my hat for me! She must have found it and put it on, and brought it all the way home for me! Now isn't that really remarkably clever? I must go and tell every one about this most extraordinary cow."

And with that Mr. Twiddle beamed all over his face, gave his wife a good slap and kissed the cow on the nose.

"Sorry, dear, sorry!" he said, as he

saw Mrs. Twiddle looking as black as thunder. "I meant to kiss you and slap the cow, I did really!"

And, clapping his hat on his head upside down, he hurried off to tell every one the story of how the cow had found his hat and worn it home. Dear old Twiddle, he *is* a muddler, isn't he!

2

MR. TWIDDLE GETS A SHOCK

Mr. Twiddle was always doing something silly. Well, did you ever hear the tale of what happened when he threw his handkerchief into the fire by mistake?

I'll tell you. It happened one morning when Mr. Twiddle was opening his letters by the kitchen fire. "You can throw the envelopes into the fire," said Mrs. Twiddle. "It will save me fetching the waste-paper basket."

Well, Mr. Twiddle at that moment felt he was going to sneeze, so, with an envelope in one hand and his best white silk handkerchief in the other, he sat in his chair, waiting for the sneeze to come.

And when it *did* come—a-TISH-oo-ish oo!—Mr. Twiddle caught the sneeze in the envelope, and threw his handkerchief, quite by mistake, into the fire!

Well, of course, he was terribly upset as soon as he had done this, and tried to rake his handkerchief out of the fire! A bit of burning coal fell on the rug and scorched a hole at once. Mrs. Twiddle came running in when she smelt the smell of burning—and how she scolded Mr. Twiddle!

"Catching a sneeze in an envelope and throwing your best handkerchief on the fire!" she snorted, pouring water on the burning rug. "Whatever will you do next, Twiddle? Don't you know the

difference between a handkerchief and
an envelope? You'll be poking the fire
with your pencil and trying to write
with the poker next! You might have
had the whole house on fire. Go out
for a walk, do, and don't come in till
dinner-time!"

Poor Mr. Twiddle! He was really
very unhappy about his best handkerchief. He got up, found his hat, put it
on back to front and went into the
village. And very soon he met old Mrs.
Gabble, who always loved a chat. When
she saw Mr. Twiddle looking so upset,
she stopped.

"What's the matter?" she said.

"Oh," said Mr. Twiddle, "a dreadful
thing happened this morning. I threw
my handkerchief on the fire by mistake,

and it got burnt, and when I tried to
get it out of the flames, some burning
coal fell on the carpet and . . ."

"Good gracious me!" said Mrs.
Gabble, "no wonder you feel upset!"
Then she caught sight of Sally Simple
and she hurried to tell her the news.

But, of course, she added a bit to it to make it even more exciting!

"Oh, Sally Simple," she cried, "have you heard what happened at the Twiddles' house this morning? Why, poor old Twiddle threw his handkerchief on the fire by mistake and, in getting it out, the fire fell on to the rug and set it all ablaze!"

"Goodness me!" said Sally, quite frightened. "And did the kitchen catch alight?"

"I expect so," said Mrs. Gabble happily. "Oh yes, I am sure it blazed up on to the ceiling!"

Sally Simple was thrilled. She longed to tell some one about the fire at the Twiddles'. She saw Dame Shoo over the way and rushed to tell her.

"Oh, Dame Shoo," she cried, "have you heard of the terrible fire at poor Mrs. Twiddle's this morning?"

"No," said Dame Shoo, startled. "What about it?"

"Oh, Mr. Twiddle dropped his handkerchief in the fire, and that started a dreadful burning," said Sally Simple. "Yes, the rug caught fire, and the flames shot up to the ceiling! The whole kitchen was on fire.

"But how dreadful!" said Dame Shoo. "I suppose the house will be burnt down?"

"Yes, sure to be," said Sally Simple. "I do wonder if the fire-engines have gone to see to it. And don't you think we ought to offer to give the Twiddles a bed for to-night, because, with their

house burnt down, they'll have nowhere to sleep!"

"Yes, yes!" said Dame Shoo. "I'll go
and tell every one else, Sally, and we'll
see what we can do."

She hurried off, longing to tell some
one the news.

On the way she passed the fire-station.
She peeped inside—and to her very
great surprise she saw the big fire-
engine still there. It hadn't gone to the
Twiddles'!

"I say! I say!" cried Dame Shoo,
rushing into the fire-station in a great
hurry. "Haven't you heard of the dreadful fire at the Twiddles' house? It will
be burnt to nothing if you don't hurry
at once!"

"First we've heard of it!" cried the

captain of the fire-brigade, and he sounded the big fire-bell at once.

In three minutes every fireman was in his place, complete with helmet. With a loud clanging of bells the great red fire-engine roared out of the building.

Clang! Clang! Clang! It sped away

to Mr. Twiddle's house. Every one ran after it to see where it was going. It stopped outside Mr. Twiddle's house. The firemen undid the long hose and looked for the fire.

Mrs. Twiddle looked out of the window. She saw the fire-engine. She saw the firemen unwinding the hose. She saw the crowds and crowds of people. Whatever had they all come for?

She opened the door and looked out.

"Hie, Mrs. Twiddle, where's the fire?" shouted the men.

"What fire?" asked Mrs. Twiddle, in the greatest astonishment.

"The fire we've come to put out!" said the men.

"Well, there's only one fire in the house and that's in the kitchen grate,"

said Mrs. Twiddle, even more astonished. "And I'm sure I don't want *that*
put out, thank you!"

At that moment Mr. Twiddle walked
up, looking as surprised as could be to
see such a crowd round his house.

"You said there was a terrible fire in
your house!" cried Dame Shoo.

"I didn't!" said Mr. Twiddle indig-
nantly.

"You did!" shouted every one.

"I only told Mrs. Gabble I had burnt
my handkerchief by mistake!" shouted
Mr. Twiddle, and he went inside and
banged the door.

The fire-engine turned round and
drove off in disgust. Every one went
home. Mrs. Twiddle stared at Mr.
Twiddle crossly.

"Do you need to bring the fire-engine here and half the town, just because you happen to have burnt your handkerchief?" she said. "Really, Mr. Twiddle! Please don't do any more foolish things today."

"Don't worry. I *shan't*!" said Mr. Twiddle gloomily, and he threw his hat into the waste-paper basket and hung up his newspaper on a peg.

Well, really, Mr. Twiddle!

3
MR. TWIDDLE FETCHES THE FISH

"Mr. Twiddle, Mr. Twiddle, the fish-boy hasn't been with the fish!" called Mrs. Twiddle. "Just put on your coat and go and fetch it for me, will you! And you might get the newspaper at the same time, because it hasn't been left this morning."

Mr. Twiddle jumped up at once. He had missed his newspaper very much, and he was pleased to go and fetch it. Yes, he would fetch the fish as well—it was on the way to the newspaper-shop.

He went off, humming, looking forward to a nice lazy morning with his newspaper when he got back. Ah, there was nothing like a good fat newspaper and a nice brown pipe! Mrs. Twiddle would be pleased with him for fetching the fish, and would let him read in peace.

He came to the fish-shop and called the man. "Can I have Mrs. Twiddle's fish, please?" he asked. "It hasn't come."

"Certainly, sir, certainly," said the man. "Five herrings, isn't it? Here they are!"

He took a newspaper, slapped the five slippery herrings into it, and rolled them up. He gave the parcel to Mr. Twiddle, who slipped it under his arm. He set off to the newspaper-shop.

"My newspaper, please," he said to the man. "You forgot to leave it this morning."

"Sorry, sir!" said the man, and he rolled up Mr. Twiddle's newspaper and gave it to him. Mr. Twiddle put it under his other arm.

Then he set off home, whistling softly. Ah, it would be nice to sit down in his

arm-chair by the fire, unfold his newspaper, light his pipe, and puff away in peace, whilst Mrs. Twiddle cooked herrings, and he smelt the delicious smell of them!

He reached home, and slapped down his newspaper on the table. "Fish, Mrs. Twiddle, fish!" he said. "Good fat herrings for dinner!"

He didn't notice that he had put his own newspaper on the table, and had put the parcel of fish on his chair. The fish was wrapped in a newspaper too, so it wasn't a difficult mistake to make.

Mr. Twiddle went to get his pipe. Mrs. Twiddle unrolled the newspaper he had put on the table. She looked astonished, and then called to Mr. Twiddle.

"Twiddle! What have you done with the fish? It isn't here!"

"Isn't there!" said Twiddle in alarm. "But it must be! I saw the man slap the herrings into the paper myself!"

"Then they must have dropped out, Mr. Twiddle," said Mrs. Twiddle crossly. "Just like you! You'd better go back and get some more."

Mr. Twiddle stared in dismay. "But I want to read and to smoke my pipe!" he said. "I'm tired!"

"Well, sit down for five minutes and rest," said Mrs. Twiddle. "Then you must go, or we will have nothing for dinner."

Twiddle sighed. Something always seemed to go wrong. He looked for his newspaper. Ah yes, he had put it in his arm-chair. The cat was there too, scraping hard at the paper. It could smell the fish in it, of course! But Mr. Twiddle didn't know that. He thought it was just his newspaper and nothing else.

"Look at the cat!" he said to his wife. "I believe she's trying to open the newspaper and read it!"

"Fiddlesticks!" said Mrs. Twiddle snappily. "Whatever will you say next? You'll tell me the canary wants to smoke your pipe!"

Mr. Twiddle lighted his pipe. Then he took up the newspaper from the chair and sat down. He shook out the paper —and out fell five slippery herrings, all down Mr. Twiddle's nice clean waistcoat and trousers!

"Bless us all, what's this!" shouted Mr. Twiddle in a fright, jumping up. "Mrs. Twiddle, Mrs. Twiddle, there's something hiding in my newspaper— big earwigs, or something! Ooo-ooo-oooh! They all jumped out at me when I opened my paper!"

The cat jumped at the fish in delight. She sat down and began to eat it. Mr. Twiddle beamed at her.

"Look at that now!" he cried. "The cat's attacking them! Clever creature!"

Mrs. Twiddle hurried in and gave a shout of dismay. "It's the herrings!" she cried. "Twiddle, are you mad? What have you given them to the cat for? Shoo, puss, shoo!"

The cat shooed. Mr. Twiddle looked

foolish. Mrs. Twiddle picked up the herrings, scolding all the while.

"Really, what shall I do with you, Twiddle! Giving me your newspaper, and trying to read the herrings, and then giving them to the cat! Well, there will be one less for your dinner now, for the cat's had one."

"I did *not* give them to the cat," said Mr. Twiddle crossly.

"You did!" said Mrs. Twiddle. "Didn't I see you beaming at the cat eating the herrings when I came in?"

"Well," said Mr. Twiddle, cheering up suddenly, "I needn't go off to the fish-shop again, because the fish are found. So I can read my newspaper in peace! Where is it?"

"Oh, I've torn it up to make new paper to line the larder shelves," said Mrs. Twiddle. "If you want to read it you'll have to go and stand in the larder and read the news on each shelf, Mr. Twiddle. That will teach you to give herrings to the cat again!"

Poor Twiddle! He spent all the morning in the larder, reading the news on each shelf, for Mrs. Twiddle had torn up the paper and spread it neatly there. He couldn't even have his pipe, for he wasn't allowed to smoke one in the larder. He really is the funniest old thing, isn't he!

4
MR. TWIDDLE AND
THE SNOWMAN

One day the children who lived next
door to Mr. Twiddle made a fine snowman in his garden. Mrs. Twiddle said
they might, because her garden was
so much bigger than theirs. So the
children were very pleased, and they
built a big man, quite as tall as their
Daddy, and very fat and round.

"Mrs. Twiddle, Mrs. Twiddle, can
we have an old hat for his head, and an
old scarf for his neck?" called the children, looking in at the kitchen window,
where Mrs. Twiddle was making cakes.

"Yes," said Mrs. Twiddle. "You'll
find an old hat in the hall, and a ragged

old scarf somewhere by it. And if you look in the hall-drawer you'll maybe find an old pair of gloves too, for the snowman's cold hands!"

"Oh, good!" shouted the children, and they tore off to get the clothes. They found them all—and they found Mr. Twiddle's stick too, which they borrowed for their funny old snowman.

My word, he did look grand when he was finished and dressed up! You should have seen him, with Mr. Twiddle's old hat on his head, a scarf tied loosely round his fat neck, raggedy gloves on his round hands, and a stick through his arm! Really, he looked very fine indeed, and the children were proud of him.

Mrs. Twiddle looked out of the

window and laughed. "He just wants a pipe to stick in his mouth," she said, "then he'll be happy. Here is one of Mr. Twiddle's."

So the children stuck a pipe in the snowman's mouth, and then danced round him, laughing. Their mother rang the tea-bell next door, and they hurried off, hungry and happy, wondering what Mr. Twiddle would say when he saw their wonderful snowman.

Well, Mr. Twiddle didn't come home till it was almost dark, for he had been to see his brother in the next village. He stumped in at the front gate, tired and hungry—and then he suddenly saw the old snowman standing quite still in his front garden.

"Hallo!" said Mr. Twiddle, in

surprise. "Who's that? What are you doing here, my good man?"

The good man didn't answer. Mr. Twiddle grew cross.

"You needn't think I can't see you, standing there, trying to hide from me in the darkness!" he said. "You are up to no good, I'll be bound! What are you waiting there for?"

The snowman said nothing at all. Mr. Twiddle marched right up to him and looked at him as closely as he could in the half-darkness. And he saw that the snowman had got *his* hat on!

"You've got my hat!" he said, in a rage. "My dear old comfortable hat! How dare you take my hat! Give it to me at once!"

The snowman didn't give it to Mr.

Twiddle. He just stood quite still and stared at him out of his big stone eyes.

"And you've got my scarf on, I do declare!" roared Mr. Twiddle. "Yes, you have! What next, I'd like to know! I suppose you've been sneaking round my house, just taking whatever you can

put your hands on! I'll fetch a police-man! I'll give you such a smack that you'll land in the next-door garden!"

The snowman stared and said nothing. "Can't you answer me?" shouted Mr. Twiddle. "Haven't you got a tongue in your head?"

The poor old snowman hadn't got a tongue of any sort, so he couldn't say a word. He just stood there in Mr. Twiddle's hat and scarf, looking very large and miserable.

"And if you haven't got my gloves and my stick!" cried Mr. Twiddle, suddenly seeing them in darkness, and feeling them. "This is too much! My hat, my scarf—and now my gloves and my stick! You are a wicked robber, and if you don't give me back my things at once, this very minute, I'll go out and get a policeman! Now!"

The snowman didn't move. Then a bit of snow melted by his mouth and his pipe fell out. Mr. Twiddle picked it up.

"And you've got my pipe too!" he shouted. "My very nicest, oldest pipe! What next! Are you wearing my vests and my socks and my best shirt under that large white overcoat of yours? Oh, you bad, wicked robber!"

Just then the village policeman came by and heard the shouting. He walked into the front garden.

"Now then, what's all this?" he asked.

"Oh, policeman, I'm glad you've come," said Mr. Twiddle. "This robber won't give me back my clothes that he's stolen. He must be deaf and dumb, for he won't even say a word to me."

Mr. Twiddle suddenly slipped on the snow and fell against the snowman. He clutched at him and one of the snow-man's stone buttons fell off and hit Mr. Twiddle sharply on the nose.

"Oh, you wicked fellow, you hit me!" shouted Mr. Twiddle, in a rage. "Take that—and that—and that!"

He slapped the snowman hard, and the snow fell off in big pieces. Mr. Twiddle was astonished. He hit the snowman again, and the funny old snowman began to fall to bits. Mr. Twiddle fell on top of him and floundered about in the snow, shouting and smacking. The policeman pulled him up, just as Mrs Twiddle came

to the door in astonishment, holding
a lantern to see what was the matter.
"Twiddle! What are you doing?"

she called. "Are you being rude to the policeman?"

"No, Mam, he isn't," said the policeman, with a grin. "He's fighting a big snowman and breaking him all to bits!"

"Really, Mr. Twiddle!" said Mrs. Twiddle, in surprise. "*Must* you do a thing like that? And look at the mess you're in! Good gracious me—and you've spoilt your new hat and broken your nice new stick! Well, you'll have to use your old ones again. The snowman has got them, so you can bring them in with you before he melts all over them."

Poor Mr. Twiddle! He couldn't think of a word to say—not a word! He went into the kitchen, all covered with snow, and Mrs. Twiddle shooed him out again.

"I'm not going to let you cover my nice kitchen floor with melting snow!" she cried. "Shake yourself in the yard, please! And chop up your broken stick—it will do for firewood!"

Mr. Twiddle went to the wood-shed very gloomily. He took the chopper— and, oh dear me, he chopped up his hat, and then went to hang his broken stick on the peg! There really is no knowing what he'll do next!

5

MR. TWIDDLE MAKES
A MUDDLE

Once upon a time Mrs. Twiddle got very tired of having Mr. Twiddle in the house.

"Mr. Twiddle, for goodness sake go out into the garden and do some work!" she cried. "Do you know what you've been doing all the morning? You've been trying to smoke your fountain pen, and you've put your pipe into the inkstand! And is it you who has stood the poker in the hall-stand and put your umbrella in the fender?"

"Oh dear! Oh dear!" said Mr. Twiddle, taking his fountain pen out of his mouth and staring at it. "I thought my pipe tasted a bit funny to-day. I'll go out and do a bit of gardening, Mrs. Twiddle."

"You'd better, before you start to poke the fire with your umbrella," said Mrs. Twiddle. "Your best one, too! Really, Twiddle, why don't you use your brains?"

Mr. Twiddle could hear by the way that his wife talked that she was not in a very good temper. So he quickly went into the hall, put on his goloshes, tied his old scarf round his neck, and ran out of doors.

It was cold. What should he do? He poked his head into the shed. It was dark there, but he could see something piled up in a corner.

"Bless us all!" said Mr. Twiddle,

staring. "I believe those are daffodil bulbs we've forgotten to plant. Dear, dear!—what would Mrs. Twiddle say if she knew all those were sprouting away there in the corner, instead of growing into nice yellow daffodils for the spring? Now, it would be a good thing if I planted them all. That would keep me busy all the morning."

So he took his spade and set to work. He dug up the bed, and then fetched the bulbs in his barrow. He set them all in nice rows, and covered them up gently with earth. Oh, he could work well when he liked, could Mr. Twiddle. He quite enjoyed himself, for the morning was fine.

He planted every single bulb, and then he heard his wife calling him.

"You seem to be working very hard, Mr. Twiddle. I suppose you will be hungry for dinner. Would you like a nice stew with carrots and onions and turnips?"

"Oooh, yes!" said Mr. Twiddle, feeling quite hungry at the thought.

"Well, fetch me a few carrots, one large turnip, and some onions from the shed," called Mrs. Twiddle. So Mr. Twiddle went to the shed and looked round. The carrots were in a basket, and so were a few turnips. He put them into a box and looked round for the onions. He couldn't see a single one. He trotted back to the house.

"There are no onions at all," he said.

"Rubbish!" said Mrs. Twiddle.

"There are heaps. Go back and look again, Twiddle."

So Mr. Twiddle went back and looked again. But still he couldn't see any onions, although this time he looked up at the roof of the shed too, thinking they might be hung there. He trotted back to the house again.

"I'm sorry, Mrs. Twiddle, but really and truly there are no onions there!" he said.

"Mr. Twiddle, you make me cross!" said Mrs. Twiddle. "Why, I put the onions in the shed myself! I'll come and show you. Really, I should have thought you knew an onion by now."

Mrs. Twiddle went down to the shed with Mr. Twiddle.

She looked all round—and then she stared in surprise.

"How strange!" she said. "How very, very strange! Not a single onion here! Where have they all gone? You haven't been eating them, Twiddle, have you?"

"Of course not," said Mr. Twiddle, offended. "I don't eat raw onions. Whereabouts did you put them?"

"In that corner," said Mrs. Twiddle, pointing. "They were there yesterday —a whole heap of them. Wherever can they have gone to?"

Mr. Twiddle stared at the corner where his wife was pointing—and a horrid cold feeling came over him. There *had* been something in that corner this morning—and he had planted it—dozens and dozens and dozens!

"What are you looking like that for, Mr. Twiddle?" asked Mrs. Twiddle, staring at him. "Have you done something to my onions?"

"Nothing very much, dear," said Mr. Twiddle, trying to smile. "I—well—I just planted them all, that's all!"

"*Planted* them, Twiddle!" said Mrs.

Twiddle, in the greatest surprise. "What did you want to plant onions for? You helped me yourself to pull them up from the ground in the autumn! Why did you plant them again?"

"I thought they were bulbs," said Mr. Twiddle.

"Well, they *are* bulbs!" said Mrs. Twiddle, "but they are not the sort to plant in the garden."

"I thought they were daffodils," said poor Mr. Twiddle. "I've been very, very hard at work all the morning, planting them in neat rows. I thought it would be such a surprise for you."

"Well, it certainly *is* a surprise," said Mrs. Twiddle. "And now, Twiddle, I'm afraid if you want any onions in your stew for dinner, you'll have to do some more hard work and dig up those onions again!"

Poor Mr. Twiddle. He sadly took up his spade and dug up all the dozens and dozens and dozens of onions he had so carefully planted that morning! And

wasn't he hungry when he had finished!
"I could eat two whole stews, I declare!"
he said to Mrs. Twiddle, when he went
in.

There was a beautiful stew for him,
and he did enjoy it.

"I'm sorry you had your work all for
nothing, Twiddle," said Mrs. Twiddle,
as she gave him a fourth helping of the

stew. "But, my dear man, do try and think what you're doing in future."

"Oh, I will, Mrs. Twiddle, I will!" said Mr. Twiddle, picking up the sugar-sifter and shaking sugar all over his stew instead of the pepper. "I've quite made up my mind about that!"

And he stirred his lemonade with the salt-spoon, smiling all over his funny old face! You just can't stop him from doing things like that, can you!

6
MR. TWIDDLE IN THE RAIN

Once Mr. Twiddle wanted to go and call on a friend of his and borrow a book. So he knocked out his pipe, put down his newspaper, and got up.

"Where are you going, Twiddle?" asked Mrs. Twiddle.

"I'm going to Mr. Twisty's," said Mr. Twiddle. "He's got a most exciting book I want to borrow—all about pirates."

"But it's pouring with rain, Twiddle!" said Mrs. Twiddle. "You'll get soaked!"

"Oh no, I'll put on my mackintosh and take my umbrella," said Twiddle. "I shall be all right."

He went into the hall, thinking about the book of pirates. He took down his mackintosh and put it on. He wasn't thinking at all of what he was doing, and when he saw his coat hanging on its usual peg, he put that on, too, over his mackintosh. Then he hunted for his umbrella.

There it was in the umbrella-stand. Good! Mr. Twiddle took it out. He went to the front door and put up his umbrella. He walked down the path— but he had got no farther than the front gate when he heard Mrs. Twiddle knocking on the window.

"What do you want?" shouted Twiddle.

"You want your *mackintosh* on!" shouted Mrs. Twiddle. "You said you would put it on! Come and do so!"

Mr. Twiddle stared down at himself in astonishment. "But I did put it on!" he called back.

"Twiddle, don't be silly," said Mrs. Twiddle, and she hurried to the front door and opened it. "Come back at once. You can see quite well you've got your overcoat on. What's the use of a mac if you don't use it when it's raining?"

Twiddle walked back, shut his umbrella, and looked for his mackintosh. Of course, as he already had it on under his coat, it was nowhere to be found.

"Well!" said Twiddle in amazement, "it was certainly hanging on its peg in the hall when I came out of the kitchen just now. Where's it gone?"

"Mackintoshes can't walk," said Mrs. Twiddle, busy looking everywhere. "Now where in the world have you put that mackintosh, Mr. Twiddle?"

Well, Mr. and Mrs. Twiddle hunted everywhere. Twiddle went upstairs into his bedroom and took everything out of his wardrobe. Then he went downstairs and out into the gardener's shed to see if by any chance he had left it there.

And whilst he was there he hung his umbrella up on a peg with all the spades and forks. But he couldn't find his mackintosh. So indoors he went again, leaving his umbrella out in the shed.

When he got indoors he wanted to use his handkerchief to catch a sneeze in. So he undid his coat and tried to find his trousers pocket—but, of course, his mackintosh was underneath and he couldn't seem to get his pocket at all.

Mrs. Twiddle looked to see what he was struggling about—and saw his mackintosh under his coat!

"Twiddle!" she cried. "If you aren't

the most tiresome man under the sun!
There's your mackintosh!"

"Where?" asked Twiddle, looking all
round him and up on the ceiling too, as
if he expected to see it flying around.

"On your own self!" cried Mrs.
Twiddle. "You put it on—and then put
your coat over it! Good gracious, I do
believe you'll forget your own head one
day and go walking off without it!"

"Well, my dear, you needn't say any
more," said Twiddle. "It was just a
mistake. After all, this hall is so dark
that it's not to be wondered at if I put
my mac on first and then my coat. Well,
I'll go. It's still raining very hard, so
I'll take off my coat and just have my
mac on."

"And what about your umbrella?"

asked Mrs. Twiddle, looking in the umbrella-stand. "Where's that gone now? You had it over your arm a few minutes ago."

"Oh, it's about somewhere," said Twiddle, looking round anxiously. Really, it was most extraordinary the way his things seemed to vanish! That umbrella was really nowhere to be seen!

"Well, I can't waste all my morning getting you ready to go out into the rain," said Mrs. Twiddle. "I've got to peel some potatoes for dinner."

She left Twiddle standing in the hall, looking everywhere for his lost umbrella. She took a basket and went out to the shed for some potatoes.

Mrs Twiddle filled her basket, and was just going out of the shed when she happened to look up—and she caught sight of Twiddle's umbrella hanging on a peg beside a spade and a fork. She stared at it in the greatest surprise. Then she went quickly into the house.

"Twiddle! Twiddle!" she called. "You must have thought your

umbrella was a rake or a hoe! You've hung it up with the tools in the shed!"

Well, really! Poor Mr. Twiddle! He stared at Mrs. Twiddle as if he couldn't believe his ears. Then, very red indeed, he went to the shed to get his umbrella. He came back with it.

He had made up his mind to be really sensible now. He would even put on his goloshes!

So he hunted for them and put them on. He did up his mac. He put up his umbrella and set off down the path just as the clock was striking one.

Mrs. Twiddle called to him. "Twiddle! Can't you see that the sun is shining hotly now and that the rain is over? You *do* look foolish in your mac and goloshes and umbrella! Also, don't you want any lunch? It's one o'clock, and I've just put it on the table!"

"Dear, dear! I've got to go without that pirate book!" groaned Twiddle. And he hung his goloshes on his coat-peg, stuck his mac into the umbrella-stand, and put his umbrella into the boot-cupboard. Do you suppose he *ever* thinks what he is doing?

7
MR. TWIDDLE'S BONFIRES

Guy Fawkes Day was coming near. Mr. Twiddle stopped and looked each morning in the toy-shop, which had a wonderful show of brightly-coloured fireworks in the window.

Now Mr. Twiddle loved fireworks— but Mrs. Twiddle didn't. She said they were noisy, bangy things that left a lot of rubbish behind them in the garden. So for many years Mr. Twiddle had had to listen to other people's fireworks, and hadn't had any of his own.

But this year he had a good idea. He would buy some for the children next door! Ah, that really *was* a fine idea!

Then Mr. Twiddle could look out of the window and see the children letting off the fireworks—and it would be as good as setting them off himself!

So on Bonfire Day he went to the toy-shop and bought a fine collection. There were six rockets, four Roman Candles,

any amount of squibs, four large Catherine-wheels, and a great many little odd fireworks that he didn't know the name of. The man put them into a big paper bag and gave them to Mr. Twiddle.

When he got home he found that Mrs. Twiddle had put on her gardening boots and coat, and was going down the garden.

"Oh, there you are, Twiddle," she said. "Put on your gardening boots too, and come along with me. It's quite time we took down the old bean-poles and sweet-pea sticks and burnt them all, along with the other rubbish. It's a fine afternoon, so it will do us good."

"Right," said Twiddle, and he put on his old boots. He went down the

garden, carrying his bag of fireworks, for he meant to hand them over the fence to the children when he saw them. He popped them into his wheel-barrow, and went to fetch his fork.

Mr. and Mrs. Twiddle worked hard. They took up all the old poles and sticks, put aside those that would do for another year, and threw the others on to the bonfire. What a lot of rubbish there was! Old stems of cut-down plants, rotten potatoes, bad apples—oh, a heap of things that badly needed burning.

"If there's one thing I do like," said Mr. Twiddle, building up the rubbish-heap, "it's a good bonfire!"

He pushed a sheet of newspaper at the bottom of the heap and set a light to it. It flared up and the bonfire began to burn merrily, for Mr. Twiddle really was good at getting bonfires going. He leaned on his fork and watched the fire.

Soon it began to die down. Mr. Twiddle called to his wife:

"Bring some more rubbish. It wants feeding a little."

Mrs. Twiddle piled some old sticks into the wheelbarrow and wheeled it to the fire. She tipped the barrow over and everything went on to the burning heap. Mr. Twiddle forked it into the heart of the bonfire.

"That's fine," he said, pleased. "My word, wife, hark at the crackling!"

But there was soon something else to listen to besides the crackling! For Mrs. Twiddle had emptied the bag of fireworks on to the bonfire too! Right into the heart of the fire they went, and Twiddle forked them well in, not knowing that they were his precious fireworks.

The flames caught hold of them. They

burnt a rocket. BANG! Whoooooosh! The rocket flew out of the bonfire like an aeroplane and took Mrs. Twiddle's hat off. She gasped and screamed.

"Twiddle! What was that? Oh, what was that?"

A shower of stars showed up at the end of the garden. It was the end of the rocket. Then BANG! Another one went off, and shot out of the fire between Twiddle's legs, knocking away his fork as it went.

"Oooooh!" said Twiddle in the greatest surprise. He jumped well away quickly as another rocket soared over his back, showering him with coloured stars!

The Catherine-wheels spluttered and fizzed. The Roman Candles exploded

with a roar. The squibs and other little fireworks went off bang and jumped out of the flames as if they were alive!

"Save us! What's all this?" screamed poor Mrs. Twiddle, jumping out of the way of a firework that seemed to want to hop on her toes all the time. "Ow! Get away, you horrid thing! Oh, there it is again! *Will* you get away?"

Twiddle stared in surprise at the bonfire. Then he suddenly guessed what had happened. Mrs. Twiddle had emptied his fireworks on the fire!

"Oh, you threw all the fireworks I bought for the children next door on to the bonfire!" he cried. "You silly woman!"

"Silly woman, indeed!" said Mrs.

Twiddle angrily. "Why didn't you tell
me you had got fireworks in your
barrow? Silly man! Very, very silly
man!"

"Well, I must buy some more for the
children," said Twiddle, jumping out of
the way of a rocket. "I'm tired of this.
I'm going in."

"Twiddle, just listen to *me*," said Mrs. Twiddle firmly. "You are *not* going to waste your money on any more fireworks. As likely as not you'll throw them into the kitchen fire and then there'd be a fine to-do! Not another penny are you to spend on fireworks. Do you hear?"

"Very well," said Twiddle meekly. He was very sad as he went indoors. Now he wouldn't be able to see any fireworks after all.

But cheer up, Mr. Twiddle! The children have bought plenty for themselves, and if only you go upstairs to your bedroom window, you'll see them all! So cheer up, Mr. Twiddle.

8

MR. TWIDDLE'S MISTAKE

At ten o'clock every night Mr. Twiddle let in the cat, and took the dog out to his kennel. If he ever forgot, Mrs. Twiddle always reminded him. The cat was usually waiting outside to come in, and the dog was usually quite ready to go out to his nice cosy kennel, lined with warm straw.

One night, at ten o'clock, Mrs. Twiddle looked at Mr. Twiddle. He was fast asleep in his chair, his head nodding over his book.

"Twiddle!" said Mrs. Twiddle sharply. "Wake up! It's ten o'clock. Time for BED."

"Ooooomph!" said Mr. Twiddle, opening his eyes with a jerk. "Er—what did you say, my dear? I wasn't asleep."

"Oh yes you were, Twiddle," said his wife, folding up her knitting. "Come along now. It's ten."

So up they went to bed, Mr. Twiddle still feeling very sleepy. He quite forgot about the dog and the cat. But Mrs. Twiddle remembered.

"Twiddle! Have you let the cat in? And what about the dog?"

"Bother!" said Twiddle sleepily, putting his coat on once more. "Well, I'll go down again."

Down he went into the dark hall. He whistled to the dog to come to him. Then he opened the door. It was quite dark outside. Twiddle felt an animal

against his legs and he thought it was the dog. But it wasn't. The dog was lying on the couch, feeling rather guilty because he hadn't answered Mr. Twiddle's whistle and gone to him. But he felt as if he would rather sleep indoors that night, because it was cold.

It was the cat that Mr. Twiddle had felt! It had come indoors and rubbed against his legs.

"Come on, come on!" said Twiddle, thinking it was the dog. He went out into the yard, where the kennel was. He couldn't see a thing, and he only knew he had come to the kennel when he bumped into it.

The cat came with him, rubbing against him.

"Go into your kennel, Tinker," said Twiddle, thinking he was talking to the dog. Usually he heard Tinker's paws running into the kennel, but he didn't hear them to-night.

So he put out his hand, touched something warm, thought it was Tinker, and pushed him into the kennel. But it was the cat he had pushed. Mr. Twiddle shut the kennel door, as he always did on cold nights. Now the dog was safe!

He went back into the house and bolted the door. He went upstairs. The dog lay on the couch, feeling very guilty and ashamed of himself, and wondering why Mr. Twiddle hadn't fetched him. And when Mr. and Mrs. Twiddle were fast asleep in bed, the dog crept upstairs to them.

He lay down under the bed, not daring to wake Mr. Twiddle. He soon fell asleep.

But Tinker always snored when he lay on his tummy with his head on his paws. And soon he began to make his little dog-snores. "Ur-r-r-r-r-r! Ur-r-r-r-r-r!"

Mrs. Twiddle woke up with a jump and sat up in bed. She listened.

"Ur-r-r-r-r!" went Tinker, dreaming of bones and biscuits.

"Twiddle!" said Mrs. Twiddle in a fright. "There's somebody in the room!"

Twiddle woke up in astonishment. He sat up too. The noise awoke Tinker under the bed and he sat up as well, and stopped snoring. There was silence, whilst all three of them listened.

"There's nobody, wife," said Twiddle crossly. "What did the noise sound like?"

"Well, it really sounded rather like Tinker snoring," said Mrs. Twiddle, puzzled. "I suppose you *did* put the dog into his kennel, Twiddle?"

"Of course I did, *and* shut the door on him." said Twiddle, settling down comfortably. "Do go to sleep, wife."

Mrs. Twiddle lay down. Tinker lay down—but he made a big bump on the floor as he did so, and in a trice Mrs. Twiddle sat up again.

"There! Did you hear that? It was a bump!" she cried. But Twiddle was asleep, so, as she heard nothing more, Mrs. Twiddle lay down. But soon Tinker began to snore again, and Mrs. Twiddle woke Twiddle by shaking him hard.

"There's that noise again!" she said. "Oh, do wake up, Twiddle! This is dreadful!"

Twiddle awoke. He felt angry. He lay and listened, but as Tinker was now awake again, he didn't snore. He was still feeling ashamed of himself because he hadn't gone to his kennel. He wanted to lick his master and mistress and say he was sorry.

Very quietly, he crept from under the bed, and sniffed till he found

Twiddle's hand hanging down by the bed.

He licked it with his warm wet tongue. Twiddle was most surprised. He simply could *not* imagine what the wetness was. He didn't like it. He took his hand away.

Tinker was sad. He went to where Mrs. Twiddle lay, on the other side of the bed. He put out his tongue and licked her nose.

"Ooooh!" squealed Mrs. Twiddle in a fright, and sat up at once. "Twiddle! Something licked me! I tell you something licked me! On my nose, too!"

"Funny," said Twiddle. "Something licked me too."

"If Tinker wasn't in his kennel, I'd think it was he who was here," said Mrs. Twiddle. "Light the candle!"

Twiddle lighted it—and at once Tinker jumped up on the bed in delight. Mrs. Twiddle gave another squeal. "What is it, what is it? Oh—it's *you*, Tinker! Twiddle, you bad, untruthful man, you said you'd put him into his

kennel. How dare you tell me such a story!"

"Well, I *did* put him there," said Mr. Twiddle, feeling as if he were in some kind of peculiar dream. "But I'm not going out to put him there again, wife. If there's a Tinker in the kennel and a Tinker here too, we've got two dogs, that's all. Goodnight!"

He went to sleep at once. Mrs. Twiddle pushed Tinker off the bed, and went to sleep as well, very puzzled and very angry.

Tinker kept jumping up on top of her, and she dreamed of elephants sitting on her all night long. Poor Mrs. Twiddle!

And in the morning, when Twiddle went to see if there *was* another Tinker in the kennel, he let out a very angry cat, who spat at him and scratched him, furious at having been shut up all the night long, when she badly wanted to hunt mice!

"It serves you right, Twiddle," said his wife, when she saw the scratch. "If you don't know the difference between the dog and the cat at night, it's just about time you learnt!"

9
MR. TWIDDLE AND THE CAT

Mr. Twiddle had a cold. He sneezed and snuffled, and Mrs. Twiddle was very sorry for him.

"You shall have a hot drink," she said, "and I will buy you some nice lozenges to suck. Now, just sit by the fire, Twiddle, and keep warm."

Twiddle sat by the fire, and toasted his legs and knees. The cat came up and purred. It loved a warm fire as much as Mr. Twiddle did.

Puss jumped up on to Mr. Twiddle's knee, and dug a claw into his trousers to hold on by. Twiddle gave a yell!

"Ow! You tiresome cat! You've

pricked me with your claw. Get down!
I've enough to do with warming
myself without having you on my
knee too!"

He pushed the cat down. Puss waited
a few minutes till Mr. Twiddle shut his
eyes and nodded—and then up jumped

Puss again. Mr. Twiddle got a shock. His pipe fell out of his mouth, and broke on the hearth.

He was very angry. "Look at that!" he said to the cat. "Now look what you've done, you careless, stupid animal! You deserve to be smacked."

Now the more Twiddle lost his temper with the cat, the more Puss seemed to want to come to him. It was most annoying. First the cat lay down on his feet, and he had to shuffle it off. Then it jumped up on to the back of his chair and tried to lie round his neck. That made him very angry.

"Are you trying to be a scarf or something?" said Mr. Twiddle to the cat. "Get down! I don't want you on my feet and I don't want you round my neck. You are a real nuisance to-night. Do leave me alone."

The cat disappeared. Mr. Twiddle went to sleep. When he woke up he wanted to read the newspaper, so up he got to fetch it.

He didn't see the cat lying on the rug, curled up in a ball. He trod on it, fell flat on his nose, and the cat leapt up and scratched his cheek. Dear me, what an upset there was! Mr. Twiddle yelled, the cat yowled and spat, and Mrs. Twiddle came running in to see what the matter was.

"Twiddle, how dare you be unkind to the cat!" she cried. Twiddle got up and glared at her.

"You just scold the cat, not me," he

said. "It's she who is being unkind to *me*! She won't leave me alone!"

He felt for his glasses. They had fallen off his nose. Mr. Twiddle went down on his hands and knees to find them. He put his hand under the sofa, but the cat was hiding there, and thought he was playing. So she patted his fingers, and made him jump.

"If that cat isn't under the sofa now!" said Mr. Twiddle. "Wife, I tell you she won't leave me alone! Take her away. I can't bear any more to-night."

Mrs. Twiddle took the cat into the scullery and shut the door on her. The cat jumped up on to the table, found Mr. Twiddle's supper there, ready for cooking, and ate it all up. Dear me, how angry he was when he heard about it!

"I'm going to bed," he said. "I can't stand that cat any more. There's something strange about it to-night. It just won't leave me alone."

"Don't be silly, Twiddle," said his wife. She got up and went into the scullery. She filled a hot-water bottle and put a nice warm, furry cover on it.

Then she went upstairs to put it into Twiddle's bed, whilst he went round the house and locked the doors.

Twiddle undressed. He grinned to himself when he thought of how he had shooed the cat out of the back door into the dark night. Now it wouldn't bother him any more. Ha ha! He wouldn't tell Mrs. Twiddle. She would be cross if she knew the cat was out at night.

He threw back the sheets and jumped into bed. He put his feet down—and good gracious me, whatever was that in the bed? Twiddle gave a loud yell, jumped out again, and glared fearfully at the lump in the bed.

"That cat again!" he said. "How did it get there? No sooner did I put

my feet down than I felt it, all warm and furry. It's a magic cat to-night. What am I to do? I simply don't dare to get into bed. I shan't tell Mrs. Twiddle. She will only laugh at me."

Mrs. Twiddle was sleeping in the spare-room bed that night, because she didn't want to catch Twiddle's cold. Her light was out. Twiddle stood in his bedroom and shivered.

"Fancy that tiresome cat thinking it would sleep in my bed!" he said to himself. "Whatever next? And I shooed it out of the back door too! Well, I shall put on my dressing-gown and spend the night in my chair in front of the kitchen fire. If that cat thinks it's going to bite my toes all night, it's mistaken!"

Poor Twiddle! He went downstairs to sit by the fire. He was almost asleep when Mrs. Twiddle appeared, looking most surprised.

"Twiddle! Whatever are you doing? I looked in your room to see if you were all right, and you weren't there!"

"I couldn't get into bed," said Twiddle sulkily. "That cat was there."

"Don't be silly, Twiddle. She never goes upstairs," said Mrs. Twiddle.

"I'm not silly," said Twiddle. "I tell you, that cat is lying in my bed, and I'm not going to sleep with it."

Just then there came a mewing outside the back door, and something scratched and scraped at the door.

"But *that's* the cat!" cried Mrs. Twiddle in surprise. "I'd know her mew anywhere! However is it that she's outside, poor darling!"

"That's not the cat," said Twiddle. "I tell you, she's upstairs in my bed, as warm as a pie."

Mrs. Twiddle opened the back door— and in bounded the cat, purring with delight. She jumped straight on to Twiddle's knee. He gave a yell.

"Get off! Wife, there must be two cats then. I tell you one is asleep in my bed."

"Well, we'll come and see," said Mrs. Twiddle, thinking that Twiddle must be quite mad. They went upstairs, and Mrs. Twiddle threw back the covers. In the middle of the bed was the hot-water bottle she had put there, warm and cosy in its furry cover!

"You thought your hot-water **bottle** was the c-c-c-cat!" cried Mrs. Twiddle, beginning to laugh and laugh. "And you went downstairs in a rage, and left your lovely hot bottle to sleep in the bed by itself! Oh, Twiddle! Oh, Twiddle, you'll make me die of laughing one of these days!"

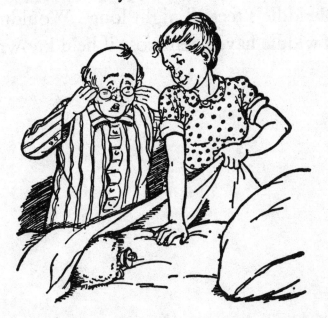

She laughed till she cried. Twiddle was angry and ashamed. He got into bed, put his feet on the hot bottle, and covered himself up.

"I'll have no more to do with that cat from now on," he said. But, dear me, as soon as he was asleep, Puss jumped up on his bed and slept peacefully on Twiddle's feet all night long. Wouldn't Twiddle have been cross if he'd known!

10

MR. TWIDDLE AND THE DOG

Once Mrs. Twiddle looked after a friend's dog for a week. It was a nice little dog, called Scamp. It was most obedient, always wiped its paws on the mat when it came indoors, and said, "Wuff-wuff" for its food.

"Really, I'm quite sorry to part with the dog," said Mrs. Twiddle, patting it. "Twiddle, will you take it back for me, please? My friend, Mrs. Gubbins, would like to have it this morning."

"Certainly, my dear, certainly!" said Mr. Twiddle. "Shall I go now? There's a bus I can catch in about ten minutes time."

"Yes—get your hat and go along," said Mrs. Twiddle. She gave the dog a biscuit, brushed his coat well, and fastened the lead to his collar.

"Dear, dear!" she said, feeling the collar. "You must have grown fatter this week, Scamp. Your collar is too tight for your neck. I'll loosen it!"

She undid the collar and slipped the buckle along to another hole. The dog liked its collar loose. It knew it could slip it off then! It licked Mrs. Twiddle's hands.

"Dear little thing," said Mrs. Twiddle. "Now, Twiddle, hurry along or you'll miss that bus."

Twiddle looked for his hat, put it on, and then, looking at his watch, he found that he only had about five minutes. He took hold of the lead and shot off down the garden-path, with the dog trotting after him. When he got to the gate Mr. Twiddle found that he had forgotten to put his glasses on. He had cleaned them and left them on the table. Bother!

"Well, never mind, I shan't really need them," said Mr. Twiddle, hurrying along. "I shall miss the bus if I don't walk fast."

Now very soon the dog met a friend. This friend was a beautiful little Pekinese, and Scamp thought she was marvellous. The Pekinese wagged her feathery tail and Scamp wagged his.

"Stop a minute and talk to me," said the Pekinese. So Scamp did a kind of double-wriggle, and slipped his head neatly out of his loose collar. He wagged his tail at the Pekinese, and joyfully licked her nose. He was ready for a jolly good game!

The Pekinese looked after Mr. Twiddle in astonishment. "Does he mind going without you?" she asked.

"I haven't asked him," said Scamp. "I say, doesn't my collar look funny running along the road without me, on the end of the lead! What will Twiddle say when he sees it?"

With a bound Scamp ran round the corner and began to have a fine game with his little friend. Mr. Twiddle didn't even see him go. He trotted along down the street, pulling the lead and empty collar behind him, whistling a little tune, and keeping a sharp lookout for the bus at the corner.

He met his friend, Mr. Jinks, who stared in astonishment at the sight of Twiddle hurrying along pulling a collar behind him.

"Where are you going?" he called.

"Just taking this dear little dog back

to its owner," said Twiddle, beaming. "Isn't it a good little soul, trotting along behind me so happily?"

Mr. Jinks thought that Mr. Twiddle must be a little mad that morning. But there wasn't any time to say so, because Twiddle hurried on so quickly. Mr. Jinks stared at the collar running along behind Mr. Twiddle, and began to laugh.

Mr. Twiddle got to the corner just at the same moment as the bus did. He jumped up, and pulled the lead and collar behind him.

"Now just go under the seat and lie down quietly," said Mr. Twiddle, peering round for Scamp. He couldn't see him, so he thought he must have gone under the seat already.

"Good dog," he said to the empty collar there. "Very good dog! Conductor, I want a twopenny ticket for myself, and a ticket for my dog."

"What dog?" asked the conductor in amazement.

"The dog with me, of course," said Mr. Twiddle. "Really, some people do ask silly questions. Don't you know a dog when you see one? Perhaps you thought I had a cat or a canary on my lead."

The conductor looked offended. He thought that if Mr. Twiddle really wanted to buy a ticket for a dog that wasn't there, he might as well let him. So he gave him a twopenny ticket and a dog's ticket as well.

A very big lady got in with a

small dog under her arm. She tried to sit down beside Mr. Twiddle.

"Madam, I have a dog under my seat," said Mr. Twiddle. "Perhaps it would be better if you took the seat over there. Our two dogs might fight."

The big lady looked under the seat and saw no dog at all. Only an empty collar. She thought it was a trick to make her take another seat and leave Mr. Twiddle comfortably alone in his.

So she sat down opposite to him and glared at him with large black eyes. Mr. Twiddle felt most uncomfortable.

"I suppose you think you are very clever," said the big lady in a freezing sort of voice.

Mr. Twiddle was astonished. He had never thought himself clever, to begin with—and he couldn't imagine why the big lady should think he did. He felt more and more uncomfortable as he sat under the glare of the lady's big black eyes, and he bent down and spoke to Scamp, whom he still thought was lying quietly under the seat.

It was dark under the seat, and Mr. Twiddle hadn't got his glasses, so he couldn't see a thing. He spoke in a quiet voice.

"Good dog, Scamp. Very good dog. Lie down quietly now."

Not a sound came from under the seat, which wasn't at all surprising.

"You do think you're funny, don't you?" said the big lady in a scornful sort of voice.

"Well, Madam, no, I can't say that I

have ever thought myself funny," said Twiddle. He got up to go, because he couldn't bear to think what the strange big lady would say next. "Come on, Scamp!" he said. "Come on."

"Mind he doesn't bite you!" called the big lady after him. Twiddle thought that was a silly remark. He jumped off the bus, and with his nose well up in the air he hurried along.

"Hie! Your dog's gone to chase a cat!" a boy shouted after him.

"Silly child!" thought Twiddle, pulling the lead behind him. "Thinks he'll make me look behind and see if Scamp really has gone chasing cats. Well, I won't!"

"Hie! Your dog's lost!" yelled another boy.

"Dear me, I wonder why children are so stupid this morning," thought poor Twiddle. "Ah—here is Mrs. Gubbins's house!"

He went up the path and knocked at the door. Mrs. Gubbins opened it.

"Oh, do come in," she said. "I

wondered if you'd bring back my darling Scamp today!"

"Then you wondered right," said Twiddle happily, pulling the collar behind him in the hall. "I've brought him—and he's been as good as gold all the time!"

He looked round to see Scamp, but the hall was dark, and he could see nothing. "He must have gone under the chest there!" he said. "Scamp! Scamp!"

"But he didn't come in with you," said Mrs. Gubbins, puzzled. "At least, I never saw him!"

"He was just at my heels," said Mr. Twiddle. "I had him on the lead."

He pulled at the lead—and the empty collar slid over the floor to Mr.

Twiddle's foot. Mr. Twiddle bent down to pat the dog that wasn't there. His hand found the empty collar and he picked it up and blinked at it.

"Good gracious!" he said. "He's slipped his collar, the rascal. Well, I'm sure he's under the chest, Mrs. Gubbins. You call him and see. I must go now or I'll miss the bus back. Good-bye, Scamp, dear little chap! Good-bye!"

He trotted off down the path again to the bus, whilst Mrs. Gubbins looked all about for a dog she couldn't find. Twiddle caught the bus and was soon trotting home down the street.

"Well!" cried Mrs. Twiddle, opening the door to him, "and where have *you* been all this time? Didn't I tell you to take Scamp back to Mrs. Gubbins for me?"

"Well, my dear, I did," said Twiddle, in surprise. "He was as good as gold all the way, and I left him safely under the chest in the hall at Mrs. Gubbins's."

"Oh—and I suppose he caught the bus back, and arrived home before you did," said Mrs. Twiddle, in a rage. "Scamp! Come here!"

And to poor Twiddle's enormous astonishment Scamp came rushing out of the kitchen, put his front paws on Twiddle's middle, and tried to reach up and lick him.

"But I've just taken you to your mistress!" cried Twiddle, sitting down in alarm. "Wife, there must be two Scamps. There really must."

"Well, it's a good thing there's not two Twiddles!" said Mrs. Twiddle with a snort. "Now *I* shall have to take Scamp home myself—and without a collar and lead too. Really, Twiddle, I've a good mind to BOX YOUR EARS."

She looked so fierce that poor Twiddle ran out to the garden-shed and sat there the rest of the day. And he still cannot think how it was that he took Scamp home—and yet found him waiting for him when he came back!

II

MR. TWIDDLE'S SPECTACLES

"Have you seen my spectacles, Mrs. Twiddle?" asked Mr. Twiddle, looking all round for them.

"Oh, dear! Have you lost them *again*?" sighed Mrs. Twiddle. "I'm getting so tired of it, Twiddle. Twenty times a day you say the same thing to me—'Have you seen my spectacles?' Why don't you keep them in the same place, whenever you take them off, then you would know where they were."

"That's a good idea," said Mr. Twiddle, blinking all round the room to see if he could find them. "But what is a safe place? Wherever I put them, they seem to disappear at once."

"Oh no they don't," said Mrs. Twiddle. "You just put them down anywhere and forget them—then you look for them in the wrong place and say they've gone. Why, I found them inside the teapot yesterday, Twiddle. Whatever made you put them there?"

"Dear me, were they really there?" said Twiddle. "Well, I wonder if they are there now."

But they weren't. Twiddle looked round everywhere, but his glasses really did seem to have vanished this time.

"When did you last take them off?" asked Mrs. Twiddle, knitting away hard.

"Let me see now—oh yes, I took them off in the bathroom when I went to wash my face," said Mr. Twiddle. "Yes, I distinctly remember doing that."

"Well, you have probably put your spectacles in the bath then, if I know anything about you," said Mrs. Twiddle. "You had better go and look."

Mr. Twiddle went—and he came back

looking rather foolish. He had his glasses on his nose.

"You were quite right, my dear," he said to Mrs. Twiddle. "I *had* put them into the bath. I suppose I thought they would be safe there whilst I washed. And, of course, I left them there by mistake."

"Now listen to me, Twiddle," said Mrs. Twiddle. "You just think of some really good place to put your glasses whenever you take them off—and *always* put them there—and then you will never, never have to look for them. You will always know exactly where they are."

"That *is* a good idea, Wife," said Twiddle, pleased. "Now where would be a good place? On top of the clock, do you think?"

"And do you think you could easily get them off the clock if you are out to tea?" said Mrs. Twiddle. "Or suppose you are at the bottom of the garden—will you like coming all the way into the house to fetch them? No—you won't. Now be sensible, Twiddle, and think of some safe place that is easy to get at wherever you are."

Mrs. Twiddle heard the back-door bell and she got up to answer it. Twiddle stood and thought about his glasses. Where would be the best place to keep them? He thought and thought—and then he smiled.

"*I* know a good place!" he said. "I'll put them into their brown leather case—and slip the case into one of my socks! Then whenever I want my glasses, all I shall have to do will be to bend down and slip the case out of my sock. Ah, that *is* a good place, to be sure!"

He put his glasses into their case, bent down and pulled up his trouser-leg—and slipped the fat brown case into the top of his sock. The suspender kept it tight. His glasses would be quite safe there. Really, that was a very clever idea.

Mrs. Twiddle called to him. "Twiddle! The fish hasn't come yet! I must go out and get it. I shan't be long."

"Very well, dear," called back Mr. Twiddle. "I'll answer the bells whilst you are gone."

Mrs. Twiddle went out. Mr. Twiddle made up the kitchen fire. He shooed the cat away from the larder. He cleaned his shoes slowly till they shone like

black polished wood. And then he felt that he really did deserve a sit-down!

So down he sat in his arm-chair. He took up the paper and began to read— but, dear me, he couldn't see to read without his glasses! So he looked on the table for them.

They were not there, of course. They were in his left sock. But dear old Twiddle had forgotten all about that. He got up and looked in his chair-seat. Sometimes he left his glasses there. But no, they were not there this time.

"Dear, dear! Gone again!" said Mr. Twiddle, really cross. "Now how am I to read without my glasses?"

He hunted all round the kitchen. He hunted all over the bedroom. He hunted everywhere—except in his left sock! Then he wondered what Mrs. Twiddle would say if she came home and found him hunting for his glasses again.

"I am sure I must have dropped them out-of-doors somewhere," said Twiddle. "I've looked simply everywhere *in*-doors. Yes—I must have dropped them in the road. Dear, dear—what a sad thing! I must put a notice in the paper to say I will give a reward to anyone finding them."

Mrs. Twiddle came back at that minute and Twiddle called to her, "I'm just going out for a minute, dear. I won't be long."

So out he went to the newspaper office. The man there said yes, he could put a notice into the paper about Mr.

Twiddle's glasses. He pushed a sheet of notepaper over to him.

"Just write down what you want us to put into the paper," he said. "What sort of glasses they are, and so on."

Mr. Twiddle took the paper and a pen. He stood and thought. Yes—he knew what to say. He would say "LOST—a nice pair of tortoise-shell glasses. Finder will be given half a crown."

He began to write the notice down— but he couldn't very well see without his glasses. He fumbled about for them in his pocket. Then he beamed. Of course—they were in his sock. He bent down, turned up his trouser-leg, and took out his spectacle-case from his sock.

He put the case on the table and

opened it. He took out his spectacles
and put them on his nose. Then he
noticed that the man was staring at him
very hard.

"Staring is rude," said Mr. Twiddle.
"Is anything wrong with me?"

"No," said the man, and he giggled.

"What's the joke?" asked Mr. Twiddle crossly. "Am *I* the joke?"

"Well—yes, in a way," said the man. "Write out the notice, please, sir."

Grumbling away to himself, Mr. Twiddle wrote out his notice. Then he gave it to the man, who read it and chuckled. He looked at Mr. Twiddle and held out his hand.

"Half a crown, please, sir," he said. "I've found your glasses for you."

"No, really!" cried Twiddle, excited. "Where did you find them? Do tell me!"

"Here they are," said the man, and he neatly took them off Twiddle's nose, put them into his case, and handed them to Twiddle. "Half a crown, reward, please."

"B-b-b-b-b-but," stammered Twiddle. "B-b-but—how did they get there?"

"Well, you took them out of your sock and put them on your nose yourself," said the man, giggling. "Now, Mr. Twiddle, pay up. It would cost you three shillings to put that notice into the paper—but it will only cost you half a crown reward. I did find them, didn't I—on your nose!"

Mr. Twiddle paid half a crown in disgust. How could he be so silly as to offer a reward to anyone finding his glasses when they were on his nose all the time!

He went home and told Mrs. Twiddle all about it. "And where are your glasses now?" asked Mrs. Twiddle, seeing that they were not on his nose.

"I expect they are in my sock," said Mr. Twiddle, and he bent down to look. But, you know, they were *not* there! Mr. Twiddle scratched his head and frowned.

"Oh dear!" he said. "Oh dear—I must have left them on the table at the paper office. Yes—that man must have got them there. Dear, dear, dear—I hope I shan't have to pay him another half-crown for finding them!"

Off he went to get them. Really, it's a wonder he ever has them at all, isn't it!

12

MR. TWIDDLE GOES OUT AT NIGHT

One night Mr. and Mrs. Twiddle were asked to go to Mr. Fankle's birthday party.

"Mr. Fankle doesn't get home till seven o'clock," said Mrs. Fankle, "so it will have to be a supper-party. Can you come?"

"We'd love to," said Mrs. Twiddle. "Only it is so dreadfully dark at night now, with no street-lamps. Still, we have our torches, and we'll come along, Mrs. Fankle. Thank you for the invitation."

"I know!" cried Mrs. Fankle suddenly. "*You* come along to tea with me in the afternoon, Mrs. Twiddle, and help me to get the supper-things ready. Then you won't need to come here in the dark. Twiddle can come along by himself quite easily, can't he?"

"Oh yes," said Mrs. Twiddle. "I'll leave all his things ready for him, and he can dress himself and come along at eight o'clock."

So, on the day of Mr. Fankle's party, Mrs. Twiddle called to Mr. Twiddle.

"Twiddle! I am leaving all your things ready for you here!" she cried. "There is your evening cloak—your top-hat—your best white handkerchief—your stick—and a parcel in which I've put your present for Mr. Fankle."

"Yes, dear," said Mr. Twiddle, not

really paying much attention. "Yes, dear. I'll remember, dear."

Now Mrs. Twiddle was calling from his bedroom, where she had laid out all the things for Mr. Twiddle. But, Twiddle thought she was calling from the kitchen, and so, that night, when he wanted to go to the party, he walked out to the kitchen to get ready.

There was nobody there. Mr. Twiddle did not dare to light a candle, because Mrs. Twiddle had not drawn the curtains before she had left that afternoon, and Mr. Twiddle knew that his wife would not have a light on unless the window was covered.

So he began to feel about for his things. Of course they were not there— they were up in his bedroom; but Mr.

Twiddle didn't think of that. He wandered round the dark kitchen, feeling here and there for his things—but, dear me! he couldn't seem to find them at all!

"Where *has* Mrs. Twiddle put them?" he said crossly. "Really, she's a very silly woman. Why didn't she put them on the table, where I could easily get them? And why didn't she draw the curtains before she went so that I could light a candle and see what I am doing?"

Mr. Twiddle didn't think of drawing the curtains himself. He just went on looking and looking. He brushed against the table, and the cloth fell on the floor. When Mr. Twiddle went walking round that side of the table again, he stumbled over the cloth.

"Ah! There's my cloak!" he said, and bent to pick it up. "Fancy Mrs. Twiddle putting it on the floor. Silly woman!"

He tried his best to put the tablecloth on like a cloak, but he couldn't. So he just wrapped it somehow round himself, and then felt about for his hat.

"That may be on the floor too," said Mr. Twiddle. "If Mrs. Twiddle put my cloak on the floor, I expect she will have put my hat there too. Dear, dear, dear!"

So he felt round the floor, and came to the waste-paper basket. It was round and tall, and felt to Mr. Twiddle just like his hat. He picked it up and put it on. Luckily it was empty.

"Seems a bit tight for me," said Mr. Twiddle, puzzled. "My head must have grown! Well, well! never mind, that's my hat found. Now for my white handkerchief."

He found a duster on the dresser, and stuffed that into his pocket, leaving a little bit of yellow hanging out. Then he hunted for his stick.

He found the poker, though he thought it felt rather heavier than usual for a stick. However, he tucked it under his arm, and was just about to go when he remembered the parcel for Mr. Fankle's birthday.

"Gracious! I nearly forgot it!" he said, and began to hunt around again for a parcel. He soon found one, though he didn't know it was only Mrs. Twiddle's old boots wrapped up to give away to the charwoman. He put it under his arm and set off, banging the door behind him.

He wore the bright red kitchen tablecloth round his shoulders, the waste-paper basket for a hat; he had a yellow duster in his pocket instead of a handkerchief, and he carried the kitchen poker for his stick. Really, Mr. Twiddle!

He knocked at Mr. Fankle's door. He was late, and every one else had arrived.

"That must be Mr. Twiddle!" cried Mrs. Fankle, and she ran to the door to open it, followed by all the others. Twiddle stepped inside. The door shut, and Mrs. Fankle switched on the light.

And then there was an astonished silence, as every one looked at Mr. Twiddle. *How* peculiar he looked!

"Well, what's the matter?" asked Mr. Twiddle, puzzled.

"Er—have you come in fancy dress?" asked Mr. Fankle, trying not to laugh.

"Of course not," said Mr. Twiddle crossly. And then he stared at the waste-paper basket he had taken off his head.

He looked at the red kitchen cloth—
and the poker. He went very red.

"Twiddle!" cried Mrs. Twiddle.
"Whatever have you dressed yourself
up like that for? You *do* look silly!"

"It was a mistake," said Twiddle,
putting down the basket, and taking off
the red cloth. He stood the poker in
the umbrella stand, and tried to look
merry and bright. He felt hot and
bothered, so he took out his handkerchief to mop his head—and pulled out
the yellow kitchen duster!

"Twiddle!" squealed Mrs. Twiddle.
"My duster! What did you take that
for?"

Twiddle threw the duster down in a
temper. Then he gave the parcel to
Mr. Fankle.

"Many happy returns of the day," he said. "Here is a little present for you."

"Oh, thank you," said Mr. Fankle, and undid the parcel. Out fell Mrs. Twiddle's holey old boots!

"Well, really, what a funny present!" said Mr. Fankle, puzzled. Mrs. Twiddle began to laugh.

"Oh, he's brought the wrong parcel!" she said. "I know what he's done, the silly man! He looked for his things in the dark kitchen instead of upstairs in the bedroom where there is a light and where I had put out all his clothes, *and* the right parcel! Oh, Twiddle! Oh, Twiddle! I shall die of laughing, I know I shall!"

And she began to laugh and laugh

and laugh. Every one else laughed too
—really, what *would* old Twiddle do
next? Who would have thought anyone would have worn a waste-paper
basket for a hat and the kitchen tablecloth for a cloak!

Twiddle stood there looking sulky
and red—and then *he* suddenly began to
laugh too. You should have heard him
—ha, ha, ha! ho, ho, ho! he, he, he!

"Yes," he said, wiping his eyes, "I'm
a silly fellow—but anyway, I've given
you a good joke for your birthday,
Mr. Fankle!" And he certainly had!

13

MR. TWIDDLE IS A FUNNY FELLOW

One morning Mrs. Twiddle wanted to make some buns and she found that she had no eggs.

"Twiddle!" she cried. "Where are you? Oh, there you are, asleep in a deck-chair in the sun as usual! Get up, lazybones, and go and do a little shopping for me."

"I wasn't asleep, my dear—I only just shut my eyes because the sun was rather bright," said Mr. Twiddle, getting up at once.

"Well, if you were awake, it's funny you should snore," said Mrs. Twiddle. "Now, Twiddle, take my basket—it's over there. And go to the grocer's, and ask for three eggs, a small bag of flour, and a pound of currants. Hurry now, because my oven is getting nice and hot for the buns."

Twiddle took the basket and hurried. He ran down the road to the grocer's. He asked for a bag of flour, which the grocer gave him. A pound of currants, and he got those too. But when he asked for three eggs, the grocer shook his head.

"Sorry, sir," he said, "but I've no eggs to-day. I may have some tomorrow."

"But Mrs. Twiddle will be very cross with me if I go home without eggs," said Twiddle in dismay. "You see she wants to make buns, and her oven is getting hot."

"That's a pity," said the grocer. "Well, look, Mr. Twiddle, sir—take some egg-powder instead. It will do quite well in place of eggs."

"All right, I will," said Twiddle. The grocer shook some yellow egg-powder into a paper, twisted it up, and gave it to Twiddle. He paid the bill, put the things into his basket, and set out again for home.

He bought some tobacco for himself, and a paper, and then stood for a moment at the gate of a field. It was full of golden buttercups, and looked very lovely.

"I think I will walk home through the fields," said Mr. Twiddle to himself. "It will do me good. And those buttercups are beautiful to see."

So off he went through the buttercup-fields. His legs brushed against hundreds of golden buttercup heads, and they shook their yellow pollen against his trousers. And when dear old Twiddle came out into the road again he found that his trouser-legs were covered with yellow powder!

"Goodness gracious! Look at that! What can it be? It's something that has fallen out of the bottom of my basket!" said Twiddle in dismay. He stared at his basket, and remembered what he had in it.

"Yes—it must be the egg-powder! It was bright yellow, I remember. The grocer must have twisted up the packet so loosely that all the powder has dribbled out of it, through the bottom of my basket and down my trouser-legs," said Twiddle. He felt rather clever to have thought all this out.

He scratched his head and thought hard again.

"I must go back and get some more. It's no good going home with an empty packet, and Mrs. Twiddle asking for eggs," he said to himself.

So back he went to the grocer's. "I'm sorry," said Mr. Twiddle, "but all the egg-powder has fallen out of the packet down my trousers. Look at it! I must have some more."

"You must have put it rather carelessly into your basket," said the grocer. He brushed all the yellow powder from Twiddle's trousers and gave him another packet, very firmly twisted up indeed. Twiddle carefully poked it down into his basket and set off again. He thought he would have time to walk through the fields again. It had been so very pleasant last time.

"The buttercups are like a big golden carpet spread out for a king to tread upon," said Twiddle to himself, and he pretended that he was the king, and walked on very haughtily, his head in the air.

And, of course, when he came out into the road again, what did he see but yellow powder all over his trouser-legs once more!

"Well, really, this is very vexing!" said Twiddle, annoyed. "The second lot of egg-powder has shaken out of the basket too! That grocer *does* pack his things carelessly."

So back he ran to the grocer's again, feeling hot and out of breath. He banged his basket down on the floor. "Look at my trouser-legs again!" he cried. "That egg-powder of yours has shaken loose from the package once

more! I've lost it all! Get me some
more, please, and put it into a tight-
lidded box this time!"

The grocer was busy and cross. He
told his boy to give the powder to
Twiddle in a box with a very tight-
fitting lid.

The boy put it into the basket,
and Twiddle marched off for the
third time. He looked at his watch
and decided that he hadn't time
to go through the fields again. He
had better run all the way down
the road!

So he set off, and arrived home very
hot and panting indeed.

"What a long time you've been!"
cried Mrs. Twiddle. "Here I've been
waiting and waiting for those things,

and my oven's so hot now that it would roast a large turkey!"

Twiddle put the basket on the table and wiped his forehead. "Now I'll just tell you what's happened," he began. "It was most annoying . . ."

"Oh, I haven't time to hear your excuses!" cried Mrs. Twiddle. "Did you bring the eggs?"

"No," said Twiddle. "There are no eggs to-day. So I brought egg-powder instead. And just let me tell you about that—the grocer was very foolish and . . ."

"Go into the garden, Twiddle!" cried Mrs. Twiddle, who was anxious to get on with her cake-making. "I'll listen to you after I've done my baking!"

Twiddle was cross. He went into the

garden and sank into his deck-chair with his pipe and paper. But he was so tired that he fell fast asleep.

But not for long! Out came Mrs. Twiddle, carrying two packets and a box, and looking very puzzled indeed.

"Twiddle! Twiddle!" she cried. "You must really be quite mad! You have brought back two packets of egg-powder and a boxful too! I shan't want so much. It is most extravagant of you!"

Twiddle woke with a jump. He stared at the two packets and the box. They were all quite full of egg-powder, fine and yellow. He stared at the yellow powder on his trousers, and he thought he must be dreaming.

"It's all right," he told his wife. "I'm

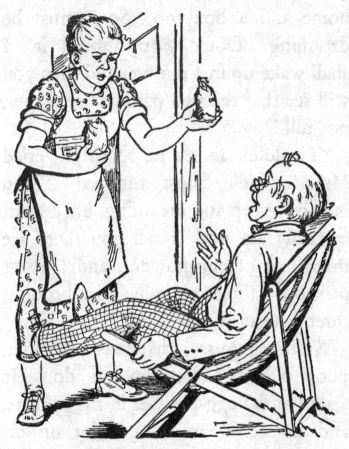

just dreaming this. I couldn't spill two
packets of egg-powder down my
trousers, and still bring two full packets

home and a box too. So I must be
dreaming. Don't worry about it. I
shall wake up in a minute, and then you
will see that the two packets are empty,
not full."

"Twiddle! Don't be so silly!" cried
Mrs. Twiddle, most annoyed. "You
may be asleep and dreaming, but I most
certainly am not! I tell you there are
three lots of egg-powder, and I INSIST
on you telling me why you brought
three instead of one."

Well, of course, that was just what
poor old Twiddle couldn't do. He
stared at the egg-powder in the packets,
and he stared at the powder on his
trouser-legs, and he never once thought
it was buttercup pollen. So how could
he explain anything to Mrs. Twiddle?

She was cross. He was upset. And the buns burnt in the hot oven. So altogether it was a most unlucky day, and only the buttercups that nodded their heads in the summer breeze knew the meaning of the puzzle!

14

MR. TWIDDLE TRIES TO HELP

Once Mrs. Twiddle twisted her ankle and couldn't get about as usual to do her work. Mr. Twiddle was very sorry for her.

"Now, my dear, you just sit down and let me run about for you!" he said. "I've got a pair of legs, haven't I? Well, I can do everything just as well as you!"

"You want brains as well as legs, dear Twiddle," said Mrs. Twiddle, sitting down with a sigh. "Oh, my poor ankle! Well well—you must do a little to help me, Twiddle, that's quite certain."

Twiddle worked quite well for a

while. He wrote out the list for the washing. He dusted the drawing-room. He fed the cat. Then he felt really tired and he sat down to have a rest.

Mrs. Twiddle called to him. "Twiddle! Twiddle! Where have you got to? There's somebody at the back door. And did you put the pudding in the oven as I told you to?"

Twiddle was half asleep. He got up at once, and, rubbing his eyes, he went to the back door. A boy was there with a clock.

"Your clock's mended, sir," said the boy, and gave Mr. Twiddle his lovely drawing-room clock. Mr. Twiddle was pleased. He had missed the clock, because it struck the half-hours and chimed the hours. It was a nice clock.

"It's the clock come back," he said to Mrs. Twiddle. "I must just put it on the drawing-room mantelpiece."

"Oh, Twiddle, I do wish you'd put the

rice-pudding into the oven first," said Mrs. Twiddle. "I keep asking you to. It won't be ready by dinner-time if you don't. Do do as you are told, if you really want to help me!"

"All right, all right, my dear," said Twiddle, still half asleep. And whatever *do* you think he did?

Why, he put the drawing-room clock

into the oven and then picked up the rice-pudding in its enamel dish and put it carefully on the drawing-room mantelpiece!

He just wasn't thinking what he was doing, of course. He shut the oven door on the clock and then went to see what else he could do.

Mrs. Twiddle hadn't noticed anything. She was knitting hard. The cat gave a mew when it saw the pudding in the middle of the drawing-room mantelpiece, but nobody took any notice of the mew. So the cat settled down and went to sleep.

After a bit the clock in the oven struck the half-hour. Mrs. Twiddle looked up.

"Why, Twiddle," she said, "that

clock is somewhere in the kitchen! I distinctly heard it strike."

"How can it strike in the kitchen when I put it in the drawing-room?" asked Twiddle, feeling cross. "You do say surprising things, Wife."

"Well, I suppose I was mistaken," said Mrs. Twiddle, knitting again.

Now, at twelve o'clock, the clock not only struck twelve times, but chimed too!

Ding, dong, ding, dong! it went; ding, dong, ding, dong!

"Twiddle! That clock is *certainly* in the kitchen!" said Mrs. Twiddle.

Well, Twiddle had heard it strike and chime as well, and he too felt sure it was in the kitchen. So he looked round, but he couldn't see it anywhere, of course.

This wasn't surprising, as it was still in the oven.

"I can't understand it, Wife," said Twiddle, scratching his head. "I distinctly remember taking it into the drawing-room."

"Twiddle, just look and see if the milk-pudding is getting on all right," said Mrs. Twiddle. "It should be doing nicely now."

Twiddle opened the oven door—and inside was the drawing-room clock, looking out at him with a very surprised face, because it was slowly cooking and didn't like it at all!

"*Twiddle!* You surely didn't put the clock to cook in the oven!" cried Mrs. Twiddle. "Oh, Twiddle—and we've just had it mended. Oh, I'm sure it will have done it no good to cook like that. You foolish man! Take it out at once!"

So Twiddle, looking very foolish, took it out and set it on the shelf to cool. It made a very peculiar noise and then stopped ticking.

"It's stopped!" said Mrs. Twiddle. "Now it will have to go and be mended again—and it's only just come back! Really, Twiddle! And what about the pudding? Did you look in the oven and see how that is doing?"

Twiddle looked—but of course the pudding wasn't there. It was most extraordinary. "I know I *put* it there!" said Twiddle. "I feel sure I did. But it's vanished."

Just then there came a knock at the front door. "There's Mrs. Harris," said

Mrs. Twiddle. "Show her into the
drawing-room, please, Twiddle, and say
I will come in half a minute. I must just
put my shoe on."

Twiddle went to the front door and
showed Mrs. Harris into the drawing-
room. He said that Mrs. Twiddle would

only be a minute. And it wasn't long before his wife was hobbling into the drawing-room with a stick.

"Good morning, Mrs. Twiddle," said Mrs. Harris. "Did you know that your cat was eating an uncooked rice-pudding in the middle of the mantelpiece? I just wondered if that was the usual place to give her her dinner."

Mrs. Twiddle looked at the mantelpiece in horror—and sure enough there was Puss lapping up the milk and the rice for all she was worth, enjoying such an unusual treat!

"Shoo, Puss, shoo!" cried Mrs. Twiddle, clapping her hands at once. The cat leapt off and upset the dish. The milk dripped into the fender and the dish fell with a clatter.

"Twiddle! Twiddle! You put the pudding on the mantelpiece instead of the clock, and you put the clock in the oven instead of the pudding!" cried Mrs. Twiddle. "Oh, it's much quicker

to do things myself! What a stupid, foolish man you are, to be sure!"

And poor Twiddle thought the same as he fetched a cloth to mop up the milky mess. "I've got to pay to mend the clock again," he thought sadly. "And I've spoilt the pudding. But never mind about that! I never *did* like rice-puddings!"

Whatever will he do next? I really can't think!